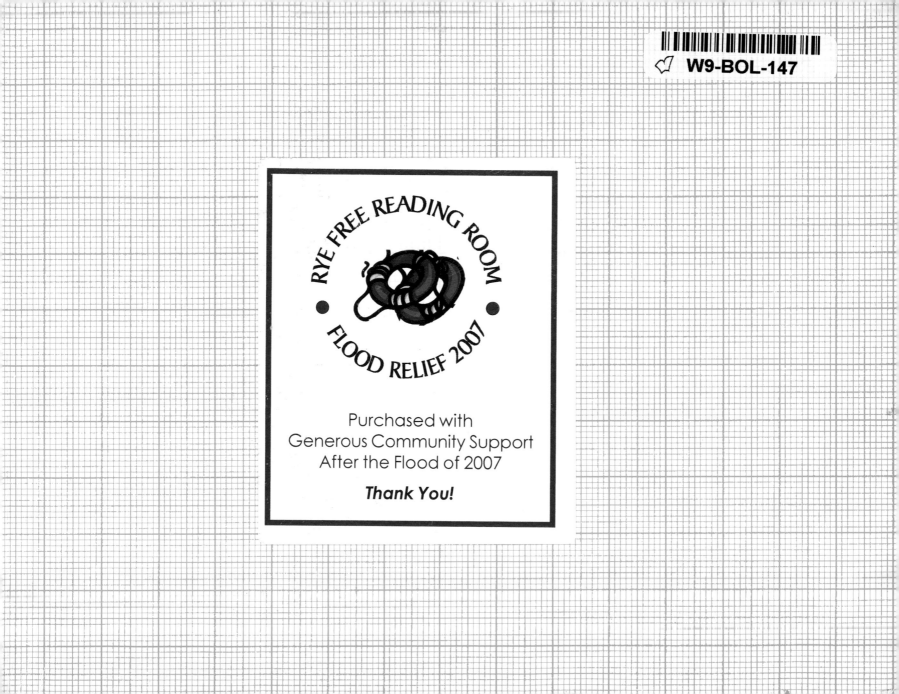

RYE FREE READING ROOM

FLOOD RELIEF 2007

Purchased with
Generous Community Support
After the Flood of 2007

Thank You!

Kane/Miller Book Publishers, Inc.
First American Edition 2008
by Kane/Miller Book Publishers, Inc.
La Jolla, California

Original Edition © La Galera, SAU Editorial, Barcelona, 2006
Original Catalan title : S'han tornat bojos!

Text copyright © Elena O'Callaghan 2006
Illustrations copyright © Àfrica Fanlo 2006

Kane/Miller Book Publishers, Inc.
P.O. Box 8515
La Jolla, CA 92038
www.kanemiller.com

Library of Congress Control Number: 2007932517
Printed and bound in China
1 2 3 4 5 6 7 8 9 10

ISBN: 978-1-933605-65-4

What's Going On?

Elena O'Callaghan
Àfrica Fanlo

Kane/Miller
BOOK PUBLISHERS

This was me before.

This is me now.

This was
my mom before.

This is
my mom now.

This was
my dad before.

This is
my dad now.

This was my room before.

This is my room now.

This was our kitchen before.

This is our kitchen now.

In the last three months, strange things have been happening around here ... *really* strange things.

My parents have been acting weird...
really, really weird.

Weird things my dad has done in the last three months:

1 He brushed his teeth with hair gel instead of toothpaste.

2 He's stopped being any good at soccer. (I can always score off him now.)

3 Yesterday, we were waiting in line at the supermarket, and he started rocking the shopping cart! Everyone was looking!

 The day before, he went to work wearing two different shoes, and he didn't even notice until he got to the office.

Weird things my mom has done in the last three months:

1 She sprayed her hair with bug spray instead of hair spray. (Actually, that was kind of funny.)

2 She put salt on the strawberries instead of sugar. (That wasn't funny. That was disgusting!)

3 She's stopped telling long bedtime stories. Now she only tells short ones.

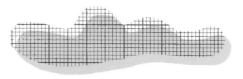

4 She doesn't pick me up
from school anymore.
Gonzalez' mom picks me up.
I can't stand Gonzalez.